Busy Bakers

Adapted by Kathryn Knight from the script by Billy Aronson

LEVEL **1** READER

Published by Dalmatian Press, LLC. All rights reserved.
Printed in Guangzhou, Guangdong, China.

The DALMATIAN PRESS name is a trademark of Dalmatian Publishing Group,
Franklin, Tennessee 37068-2068. 1-866-418-2572.

Riiiiing!

"Hello. This is baker Ernie.
How can I help you?"

Mumble mumble grumble.

"Your name is Big Bob
and you want fruity gloop?"

"We make pies. We bake cakes,"
said Bert. "We do not make gloop."

Mumble mumble grumble.

"Oh! Then you want ten pies,
one small, small cake,
and one tall, TALL cake?"
said Ernie. "Okay, Big Bob!"

"Ernie!" Bert cried. "That is a lot!
We cannot make all that!
Bob will be mad, and Bob is BIG.
We must hide!"

"We cannot hide behind a pie!"
Ernie giggled. "Heh heh heh."

"Okay, Ernie," said Bert.
Bert got a big cookbook.
"Then we will do our best."

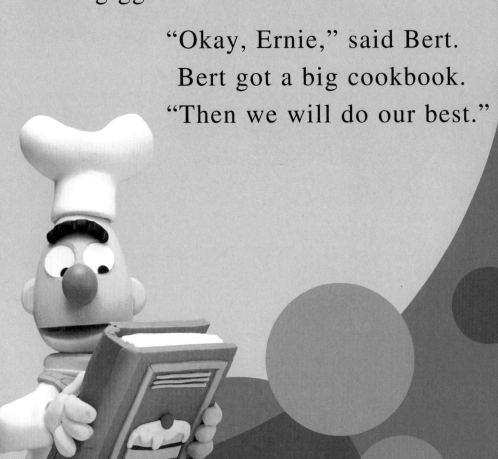

Bert looked in the book.
"To make cake,
get some water."

"Okay," said Ernie.
He got a **lot** of water.

"Get some cake mix,"
said Bert.

"Okay," said Ernie.
He got a **lot** of mix.

"Get some poof powder,"
said Bert.

"La-la-la!" sang Ernie.
He got poof powder.
He got a **lot**!
He mixed and mixed!

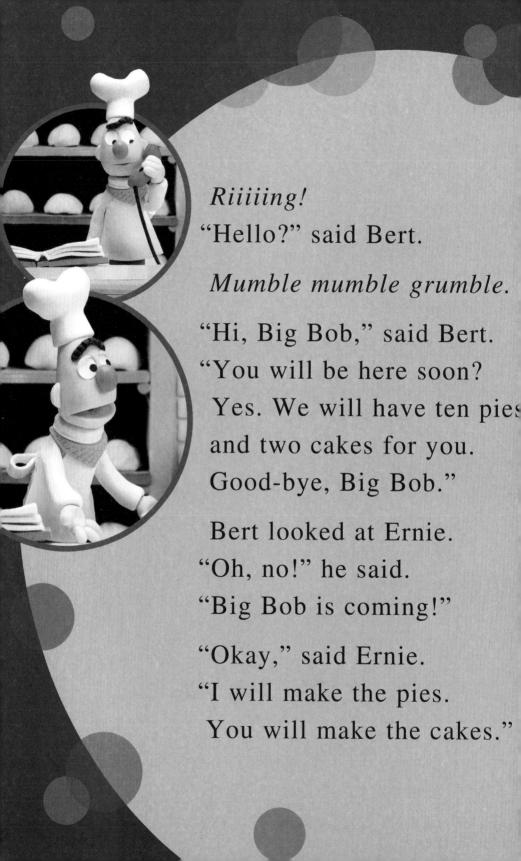

Riiiiing!

"Hello?" said Bert.

Mumble mumble grumble.

"Hi, Big Bob," said Bert.
"You will be here soon?
Yes. We will have ten pies
and two cakes for you.
Good-bye, Big Bob."

Bert looked at Ernie.
"Oh, no!" he said.
"Big Bob is coming!"

"Okay," said Ernie.
"I will make the pies.
You will make the cakes."

Ernie went to the pie machine.
He pushed the SLOW button.
The pies went past Ernie.
He put in apple bits.
He put in nuts.

"This is too slow," said Ernie.
He pushed the FAST button.
The pies zipped past . . . fast!
Apples! Nuts!
Apples! Nuts!
Apples! Nuts!

Zip! Zoom!
The pies
zipped away!

Bert made a tall, TALL cake.
"Now I will make the
small, small cake," he said.
He looked at the cake batter.
Oh, no!

"Ernie!" Bert yelled.
"You put in too much poof!"

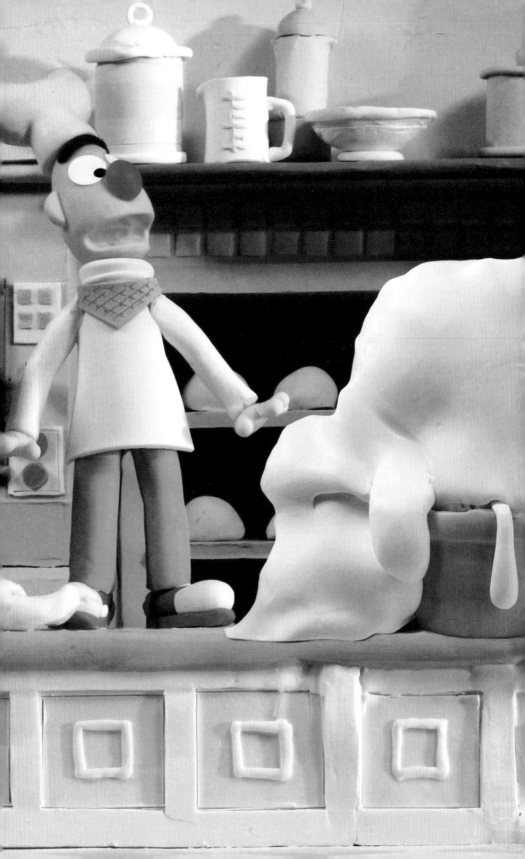

Ernie ran in.
Zip! Zoom!
Pies zipped in!

Drip! Slip! Slop!
Batter dripped out.

Riiiiing!
"Hello?" said Ernie.

Mumble mumble grumble.

"Hi, Big Bob," said Ernie.
"You will be here **very** soon?
Good-bye, Big Bob."

Zip! Zoom! Drip! Slip! Slop!
Ernie jumped away—
SPLAT!
—right into the batter.
Ding-dong!
The doorbell rang!

"I am here!"
called Big Bob.
"Open the door!"

"Okay!" called Bert.

Bert and Ernie got out
of the batter.

Bert went to the door
to see Big Bob.

Bob was not TALL.
Bob was not big at all.
Big Bob was small.

"Did you make my
ten pies?" he asked.
"Did you make my cakes?"

"Well . . ." said Ernie.
"Um . . ." said Bert.

Slip! Slop! Blub! Glub!
A big blob of batter
dripped to the door!
"We made a mess,"
said Bert.

Big Bob looked.
Big Bob smiled.
"No," he said.
"You made fruity gloop!"

"We did?" said the bakers.

"Mmmm! Yes! It's good!"
said Big Bob. "I want
ten more . . .

. . . made the same way!"

"Oh, no . . ." said Bert.

"Heh heh heh!"
Ernie giggled.